"Mission 2: Supersonic" was originally published in English in 2007. This edition is
published by an arrangement with STRIPES PUBLISHING, an imprint of Magi Publications.

Darby Creek
A division of Lerner Publishing Group, Inc.
241 First Avenue North
Minneapolis, MN 55401 U.S.A.

Website address: www.lernerbooks.com

Library of Congress Cataloging-in-Publication Data

Zucker, Jonny.
Supersonic / by Jonny Zucker ; illustrated by Ned Woodman.
pages   cm. — (Max Flash ; mission 2)
Originally published in the United Kingdom by Stripes Publishing, 2007.
Summary: "Max's second mission is out of this world! The DFEA tells Max that there's
a vicious alien race preparing for a revenge attack on Earth, and he must blast off into
space to defend the planet. Has Max got what it takes to battle evil aliens and save his
fellow humans from slavery?" —Provided by publisher.
ISBN 978-1-4677-1208-8 (lib. bdg. : alk. paper)
ISBN 978-1-4677-2052-6 (eBook)
[1. Human-alien encounters—Fiction. 2. Outer space—Fiction. 3. Adventure and
adventurers—Fiction.] I. Woodman, Ned, 1978– illustrator. II. Title.
PZ7.Z77925Sv 2013
[Fic]—dc23   2012049020

Manufactured in the United States of America
1 – BP – 7/15/13

MISSION2

SUPERSONIC

Jonny Zucker

Illustrated by
Ned Woodman

MAX FLASH MISSIONS

CHAPTER 1

The sword came crashing down towards Max Flash. Max thrust out his cutlass and managed to block the powerful blow.

But it only held off the Ninja Baboon for a few seconds.

Immediately, the creature smashed the sword towards Max's knees. Max leaped into the air. The weapon swished just millimeters below his body.

The Baboon shrieked with frustration. It threw its sword onto the craggy ground. It beat its chest in fury. Orange wisps of smoke poured out of its nostrils. Shoots of stinking grey spittle flew out of its mouth.

Max tightened his grip on the cutlass. He quickly scanned the darkened graveyard.

What should my next move be?

The Baboon breathed heavily. It raised its giant fists. It began to advance towards Max.

And then Max saw it—the Orb of Justice.

It was resting on top of a streetlamp just beyond the graveyard wall. It glowed with a flickering pulse of green light.

If I can outrun this monster, maybe I can make it to the Orb. The Ninja Baboon will be no match for the Orb's incredible powers.

Max suddenly remembered the smoke grenade in his pocket. In an instant he pulled it out. He hurled it toward his enemy. The Baboon howled in terror. It began to back off. Max started to run towards the Orb. He didn't look back until he was halfway across the

graveyard. He immediately wished he hadn't looked.

The Baboon's initial fear of the grenade had disappeared. The monkey was now thundering after Max. It was only a few yards behind him. Max upped his pace frantically. When he was fifteen feet from the Orb he leaped into the air. Max reached out to grab the prize. Just as he made contact with it, he felt the Ninja Baboon's claw on his left ankle. He froze in mid-flight.

A second later, all signs of the Baboon, the Orb, and the graveyard completely vanished. Max spun around. He was back in the living room. His mom was striding towards him. She had a serious expression on her face.

"Mom!" he protested loudly. "If I'd got the Orb I'd have made it to level 7!"

"You can play computer games again later. Zavonne wants to see you," she said.

Max arched his left eyebrow and put his

electronic control sword down on the table.

Zavonne? Is it time for my second mission?

CHAPTER 2

Max had met Zavonne only recently. His parents had introduced them. Without a shadow of doubt, meeting Zavonne had been the biggest shock of his life.

Max's mom and dad were a stage magic double act. Max had grown up backstage in theaters. He watched his parents. He watched a whole range of other magical acts. He studied their tricks. He worked out how they were done. Then Max perfected them himself.

Max had more than just stage-magic abilities. He was remarkably double-jointed. This helped him squeeze in and out of incredibly tight spaces and perform astounding feats of contortion.

Just over a month ago, his parents had taken him to a secret communications center under their cellar. A woman called Zavonne had appeared on a screen. She told Max about the organization she worked for—the DFEA. It stood for the Department for Extraordinary Activity.

She'd said that the DFEA dealt with "unusual" activities. Things that would freak out the normal forces of law and order. Things like time travel. Things like creatures from outer space. Max learned that his parents had carried out two DFEA operations in the past. Zavonne then told him his own skills made him a perfect choice to be a DFEA operative.

Zavonne had gotten Max's help in fighting a computer game character called Deezil. Deezil was a terrifying lizard man. He had been determined to break free from the Virtual world. He was going to imprison his creators—humans. Max had been transported into the hard drive of a top programmer's computer. There, he took on crazy racecar drivers, bloodthirsty soldiers, and gross slimy beasts. This was all on his path to stopping Deezil's evil plan. It had been a totally crazy, terrifying, and brilliant adventure. Max grinned at the thought of a second mission.

Max's dad waited for Max and his mom. He stood at the top of the steps leading down to the cellar. The three of them walked down into the dim light. Just like before, Max's dad flicked a switch that moved a workbench over against a wall. This revealed a small panel in the floor. He slid the panel aside. He stood back.

Max looked at his parents' concerned faces. They'd come down with him to the communications center the first time. Now, he was a fully fledged DFEA operative. He was to meet with Zavonne alone now.

"Good luck," said his mom.

His dad squeezed Max's shoulder. He gave him an encouraging smile.

Max lowered himself onto the ladder. His feet hit the floor at the bottom. He flicked on the lights.

The communications center was a square room. The walls were dotted with hi-tech equipment and digital display panels. There were racks of red levers and green buttons.

On the wall across from Max was a giant plasma screen.

It suddenly came to life. Zavonne's face appeared. She looked as ice-cool and unsmiling as the last time he'd seen her.

"We have a situation," said Zavonne briskly.

Great to see you too! Max thought sarcastically.

"It's connected to outer space," she continued. "Get ready for blast off, Max."

CHAPTER 3

Max stared at Zavonne.

Outer space?

Zavonne stared back without emotion.

"Forty years ago, a UFO landed in a remote area deep in the countryside," she began

Max had read lots of stuff about UFOs. He had never seen anything that offered any hard evidence that they existed. Although, he'd always assumed it was impossible to be sucked into a computer's hard drive. Until he'd done it himself, that is.

"The equipment the authorities use to monitor the skies was too unsophisticated to pick up this craft," Zavonne continued. "But the DFEA spotted it. We rushed a team out to see if it was a manned or unmanned flight. Onboard was a group of aliens. We saw they meant us no harm. They were, in fact, sick. They were incredibly weak. The first problem was understanding what they were trying to tell us. It took over a week to make equipment that was complex enough to communicate with them. Once we built the Speech Pulse Translator, DFEA operatives could finally understand what these aliens were saying. And they could understand what we were saying. The first thing they told us was that they were from the planet Zockra."

"Never heard of it," said Max.

"That's because Zockra exists in a galaxy beyond our solar system. The Hedra galaxy can only be entered through a tiny vortex.

Conventional astronauts and space scientists know nothing about it. There are many planets up there. Most of them are inhabited by small groups of aliens."

"Why were the Zockrans so ill?" asked Max.

"Humans were producing massive amounts of pollution. The chemicals and gases rose up through the hole in our ozone layer. The gases slipped through the vortex and into their galaxy. Other alien groups were not affected by these pollutants. But the Zockrans were being poisoned. They came to Earth in a last-ditch cry for help. They journeyed to the source of the pollution. They exposed themselves to a massively strong dose of poison to try and find a cure. The DFEA took the Zockrans in. They looked after them in a top secret laboratory. They tried to figure out how to save them."

Max was stunned.

"And did you?" he asked.

"We did lots of experiments. We eventually

discovered that humans have something called Aura Energy. This energy slows down the poisoning process from the pollution. Without this energy, we'd all be dead by now. No one outside of the DFEA knows this energy exists."

"So the Zockrans needed some of this Aura Energy stuff?" said Max.

"Yes. But the problem was how to transfer the energy to them. The Zockrans were getting worse fast. If we didn't work it out quickly, they'd all die."

"So what happened?"

"Late one night, DFEA engineers had a breakthrough. They discovered that Aura Energy could be transferred from humans to Zockrans with a device called a Re-Energizing Pod."

A small inset box appeared on the screen. It showed a metal cage with a domed top.

"A human enters one of these Pods," said Zavonne. "Then an Aura-Energy transfer can

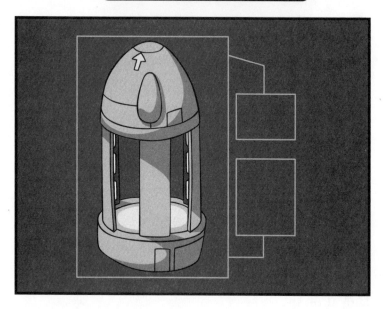

take place. As long as Zockrans are within a hundred meters of the area. The more humans involved, the greater the amount of energy transferred. For the Zockrans to stay "refreshed," these transfers have to take place frequently. DFEA engineers also learned that the Re-Energizing Pods need to be deactivated before reaching the Critical Point. For an average adult, that point is reached after five minutes."

"Is that all?" asked Max.

"Yes," replied Zavonne. "Five minutes is enough. As long as the human spends no more than five minutes in a Pod at a time, this process can be carried out without causing the slightest pain or danger to that human."

"Cool," whispered Max.

"Anyway," continued Zavonne, "when the Zockrans were fully recovered, they told us they wished to return to Zockra. We agreed that a ten-person DFEA Unit would travel with them. They would bring along ten of these Re-Energizing Pods. The members of this unit would spend six months on Zockra. They would use the Pods to transfer Aura Energy. This made sure the Zockrans stayed in good health. When the unit finished their six-month tour, they would return to Earth. They would be replaced by another ten-person team, and so on. That way, Zockran survival would be guaranteed."

"Wouldn't it be easier just to stop humans from polluting so much?" asked Max.

Zavonne gave him a hard stare. "What do you think environmentalists spend their lives doing? Humans are constantly warned of the effects of global warming. They choose to ignore the warning."

"Point taken," Max said with a nod. "But did the Zockrans do anything for the DFEA in return?"

"They did," replied Zavonne. "The Zockrans promised they would act as an early warning system if any hostile alien race planned an attack on Earth. They made a commitment to defend our planet if war did break out."

"Is that why I'm here?" asked Max. "Are we about to be attacked?"

"We strongly suspect so," replied Zavonne. "We just received a distress signal from the Zockrans. Last night, planet Zockra was invaded. The current DFEA Unit was

kidnapped. This has had an immediate effect on the Zockrans' health. They're in critical condition."

"So you're sending another DFEA Unit up there?"

"No, Max," replied Zavonne. "We're just sending you."

CHAPTER 4

"You're sending me alone?"

"That is correct."

"But why me? Why not an adult DFEA operative?"

"One of the reasons I recruited you in the first place was your exceptional agility and contortionist skills," Zavonne explained. "I believe those qualities will be central to this mission. That's why I've selected you above an adult operative. We don't know what we'll be dealing with up there. Your special

skills may give you the edge in a dangerous situation."

"OK," Max agreed. "But there are ten people in the DFEA Unit. The combined Aura Energy they transfer will surely be greater than the amount I can give."

"That's true," said Zavonne. "But you'll be able to provide enough energy to keep the Zockrans alive until the kidnapped unit is found and freed."

"How long will my energy transfer last?"

"We have been looking into this," replied Zavonne. "An adult can stay in a Pod for up to five minutes. DFEA engineers have figured out that a child should only stay for two minutes. You must leave the Pod when those two minutes are up. Failure to do so could be life-threatening. Do you understand?"

Max nodded as Zavonne pressed on. "We can get you to Zockra incredibly quickly in one of our spaceships. The speed you'll be traveling at is so fast that no radar on Earth will be able to pick it up. But before you set out, you'll need to complete a brief training. You must go to the DFEA's hidden Space Base immediately. There is no time to lose."

MAX FLASH MISSION 2

CHAPTER 5

Max's dad checked his rearview mirror. There was no other car in sight. They'd been driving on an empty country road for just under an hour. They followed Zavonne's instructions to the letter.

"Be careful," he said. He looked worried. He gave his son an affectionate squeeze on the shoulder. "We want you brought back to Earth as quickly as possible."

Max gulped nervously. He got out of the car. He stepped over to a very tall bunch of

shrubs at the side of the road. He climbed up
the bank. He stepped past the large patch of
daffodils. Max dipped his head and walked
straight into the hedge. Feeling around with
his right hand, he finally found the small metal
dial. Max twisted it to the left as Zavonne had
instructed.

Instantly the hedge parted, leaving a very
narrow gap. Max turned around and waved.
Max slid through the opening. As soon as he

was past it, the hedge slid
shut.

In front of him was
a long path that cut
through some trees. Max
hurried forward. He saw
a stone square on the
ground in front of him.
The stone began moving.
It revealed an opening.
Max stepped forward.

He slid down a chute into total darkness. He crashed into a room a few moments later. He picked himself up. A series of spotlights came on. They lit up a line of arrows leading into the distance. Max followed the arrows. He reached a high, steel door.

What shall I do? Hang around until someone comes? Or knock?

He'd just raised his left fist to knock when a panel in the door opened. A man wearing a dark green jumpsuit and a radio headset appeared.

"Operative Hunter," said the man, introducing himself. "You must be Max."

Max nodded.

"We need to get straight to work," said Hunter. He showed Max through the door and down a narrow, dimly lit corridor. Max struggled to keep up with Hunter. He heard strange noises all around him—twisting metal, grinding machines, and whirring motors.

Finally Hunter stopped in front of a door on the left. He swiped some sort of card and disappeared inside. Max followed and found himself in a whitewashed room. It was as large as an aircraft hangar.

Around the walls were hundreds of pieces of shiny equipment. They gleamed under bright lights. They were in all shapes and sizes. Some were no bigger than a football.Others were at least thirty meters high. Each piece was covered in buttons and levers.

"Unreal!" murmured Max.

"Right," said Hunter briskly. "The Zockrans are deteriorating rapidly. We need to get you up there fast. But as Zavonne explained, I need to give you a crash course in space survival."

Max listened anxiously.

"First, we need to fit you with a spacesuit."

Hunter pressed a panel on the wall. A long metallic arm shot out. It held a perfectly folded

garment. Hunter lifted it off. He passed it over to Max.

"It goes over your clothes and MUST be worn at all times in space," said Hunter.

Max excitedly slipped on the spacesuit. He wondered whether he could smuggle it home after the mission.

"The helmet is operated by that little green button on your chest."

Max pressed the button. A see-through helmet flipped out from the back of the suit and over his head. Hunter motioned for him to put it back down. Max pressed the button again. The helmet snapped back into place.

"And now for your weightlessness training."

Hunter pointed to a glass door that faced a large open space. It was surrounded on all four sides and on its ceiling by mesh. Max grinned.

Of course! Floating in space. How cool!

He went through the door, which immediately closed behind him. Max stepped onto the large mat that ran across the entire floor. Before he'd made it to the center of the mat, he heard a loud whooshing sound. He was lifted upwards.

Instinctively he pawed at the air. He tried to paddle himself back to the ground. But after

a few seconds, he relaxed a bit. He let himself
get used to the feeling of zero gravity.

A minute later, Max was having the time
of his life. He was flipping his body over. He
shimmied from side to side. He hurled himself
in every direction.

*This is wicked! We have to get one for the
school gym!*

After five minutes, the whooshing sound
began to fade. Max felt himself slowly falling

back down onto the mat. He made it to the bottom. Max exited through the glass door. There, Hunter was waiting for him.

"Now I need to give you a crucial chip," said Hunter. He retrieved a tiny chip from one of his jumpsuit pockets. "This is a receiver/transmitter for your Speech Pulse Translator, or SPT, attachment. It'll ensure that you understand any creature you come across. They will understand you in return. I'm just going to place it in your right ear. You won't feel anything."

The chip was painlessly placed within seconds.

"Now I need ten minutes to show you the flight simulator."

They sat down together in an exact copy of a spaceship's cockpit. "Your craft has just been serviced," said Hunter. "Malfunctions—although they do happen—are very, very rare."

Well that's reassuring! thought Max.

Hunter started explaining the huge array of buttons, switches, and levers in front of him. Max's brain was soon reeling. There was no letting up. Max thought he had understood the

functions of the control panel. He was allowed to "fly" the craft alone. Then Hunter produced an interstellar map. He began to guide Max around the Hedra galaxy.

Finally, he paused.

"Have you got all that?" he asked, looking concerned.

"Er . . . kind of," Max replied.

"Good," said Hunter. "Now it's time for your gadgets."

CHAPTER 6

Max's eyes lit up.

Gadgets! Bring them on!

Hunter reached into his jumpsuit. He pulled out three items. He placed them on a white table to Max's left. Hunter picked up the first one. It looked exactly like a small roll of tape.

"This is what we call a Direct Passage Pulverizer. Pull out a short length of tape, stick it to the surface of a wall, and hold the rest of the roll in your hand. Immediately, you and the section of wall you stuck the tape on will be propelled forward at astonishing speed. Your momentum will smash through any type of obstacle. It will keep going for fifteen seconds. It's quite a white-knuckle ride."

Max nodded. He placed the tape in one of the pockets of his spacesuit.

"Next is a Zing-Board," said Hunter. He handed Max a tiny silver skateboard. It was no bigger than the one Max had in his version of Monopoly.

"I don't think this will get me very far," Max said doubtfully.

"There's a tiny blue button underneath this Zing-Board," replied Hunter. "If you press it, the Board extends to full size. It will travel on any surface at the speed of sound."

"Brilliant!" said Max. He turned the Board over in his hands. "Can I keep it when I'm back on Earth?"

"You know the rules, Max," Hunter said with a stern look. "Each gadget can only be used once."

Max grimaced. His friends would go crazy over that Board.

"Your third gadget is called a Net Can."

Hunter picked up an ordinary-looking drink can.

"Peel back the top," he explained, "and whoever is standing directly in front of you will be instantly wrapped

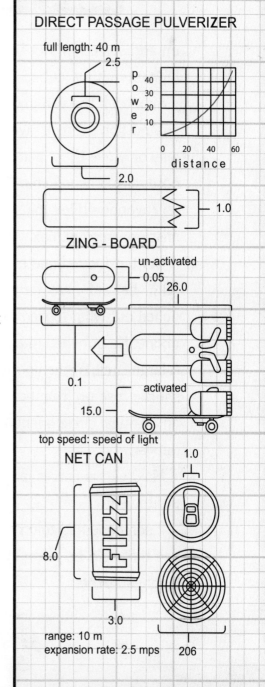

DIRECT PASSAGE PULVERIZER

full length: 40 m

2.5

power

40
30
20
10

0   20   40   60

distance

2.0

1.0

ZING - BOARD

un-activated

0.05

26.0

0.1

activated

15.0

top speed: speed of light

NET CAN

1.0

8.0

3.0

range: 10 m
expansion rate: 2.5 mps

206

up and sealed in a tight net made of the highest quality, cut-resistant rope."

Max took the can and pocketed it carefully.

"And don't forget," warned Hunter, "you may only use these gadgets when absolutely necessary or when your life is in danger."

"Zavonne drilled that into me on my first mission," replied Max.

Hunter nodded and checked his watch. "OK," he said. "We're right on schedule." He pulled out what looked like a very slim cell phone. He punched in a sequence of numbers. A large circle of the floor slid open. A space shuttle rose up from below. At the same time, an identical circle opened in the roof of the hangar.

Max felt his nerves jangle with tension and excitement.

If someone had told him a few months ago that he'd be going into space, he'd have laughed at them.

"As Zavonne mentioned, we can get you to Zockra incredibly fast in this craft. The flight panel inside looks exactly the same as the simulator you tried out. Remember, you will be flying on autopilot. Just sit back and enjoy the ride."

"Right," said Max. He swallowed nervously.

Hunter stuck out his right hand. They shook. "Good luck, Max," he said. "I'll see you on your return."

Max walked over to the flight of stairs that led up to the cockpit. He climbed to the top. Max took a quick look around. Hunter was at a large console. He flicked a whole series of flashing switches.

The door of the craft swung open. Max stepped inside. The cabin was circular. As Hunter had told him, the flight panel was an exact replica of the simulator. Max sat down on the low, black chair. Two steel seat belts eased out from the wall. They dropped over his shoulders and clicked tightly into place.

Hundreds of yellow and blue dials flashed on the flight panel in front of him. The noise of rumbling engines flooded the cabin a few seconds later.

Max felt his pulse racing.

I cannot believe what is about to happen. I'm going into space!

He saw a digital display appear on the flight panel with the number 5. He quickly flipped on his helmet. As the cabin started to rock, Max closed his eyes and began to count.

5, 4, 3, 2, 1, liftoff!

The cabin suddenly shot upwards. Max's stomach flipped. His whole body shook from the sheer speed of the craft.

This is insane!

After a few minutes, the shuddering disappeared. It suddenly felt like the shuttle had stopped. Max realized that he must be outside Earth's atmosphere.

After half an hour had passed, the shuttle slowed down. A hissing noise filled the air outside. The craft went slower and slower. It finally juddered to a halt.

Have I arrived at Zockra already? thought Max, amazed. The seat belts retracted. The door shot open. Muggy air drifted inside the cabin.

Max took a very deep breath and stood up. He flipped off the helmet of his spacesuit. He walked through the cabin door.

He immediately regretted this move.

The most bizarre thing he'd ever seen was coming toward him. It had a long, thin body and an oversized head. Max's jaw dropped as he saw its four eyes and a mouth that looked like a half-circle of green jelly. It had ten extra-long fingers on each hand. It was wearing a tiny peaked cap on its head. It wore a pink suit that was at least five sizes too small.

"Hey dude, don't freak out!" cried the creature, seeing the look of horror on Max's face. "I'm the welcoming party!"

MISSION2

CHAPTER 7

The welcoming party was an alien called
Arcan who worked for the Inter-Planetary
Rail Company. He drove a vehicle called a
Planet Hopper. It looked a bit like a hi-tech
underground train, but with just two
carriages. One carriage for him and one for
the passengers. He'd invited Max to sit up
front with him. They were already speeding
past dazzling planets, giant star formations,
and weird multicolored moons. Max was glad
that the Speech Pulse Translator was working.

Without it, he and Arcan would be feeling very confused.

"The Zockrans sent me to pick you up," Arcan explained. "You touched down on a Hedra Docking Station. Your shuttle will be fine there. I'm taking you to Zockra."

Arcan's green jelly mouth suddenly turned up with pride. "I've had most types of creature in my Hopper. I've never had an Earthling. This is far out!"

"Yeah," nodded Max nervously, "this is DEFINITELY far out."

"The Zockrans are in a bad way, my friend," said Arcan, suddenly looking very serious. "I heard about the kidnapping of that Earth crew. Bad news, dude, very bad news. The Zockrans are still alive. They desperately need some of that Aura Energy. I guess you've come to fizz them up a bit?"

"That's right," said Max. "I'm going to do an energy transfer. But I need to get there fast."

"No problemo, kid!"

Arcan kicked the accelerator pedal. The Hopper scorched forward. Max noticed a thin black cord above his head. He grabbed it to steady himself.

After a few minutes of high-speed flying, Arcan hit the brakes on the Hopper. He hovered down towards a yellow planet that was covered with tiny lakes.

"This is Zockra, amigo," said Arcan, "and that building over there is the Command Center."

The doors of the driver's carriage sprang open. Max held out his hand for a handshake. One of Arcan's long fingers shot forward and wrapped itself around Max's hand. Arcan then held out another finger. This one was holding a tiny strip of silver. "This is a Hopper Hurry Card," he explained. "Press this side, and I'll come and pick you up from any place in the Hedra galaxy."

Max thanked him. He tucked the silver strip into the pocket of his spacesuit.

"Thanks for the ride, Arcan. Maybe I'll see you around."

"I'm sure you will," grinned Arcan.

Max stepped out of the carriage. Arcan flicked the doors shut. The sticky yellow goo

on the ground sucked at the soles of Max's boots.

The Hopper flew out of sight. Max studied the Command Center for a few seconds. He was about to head for the door when he heard a strange hissing sound behind him.

He turned around. Max saw a silver-and-purple spaceship hurtling straight for him.

CHAPTER 8

Max looked around in panic. There was no time
to run. The craft thundered nearer. He spotted
a tiny metal slot on the ground. The spaceship
was almost upon him. He acted immediately.
Forcing his feet off the sticky yellow goo, he
threw himself downwards. He just managed
to squeeze himself through the narrow bars
of the grille. The spaceship crashed forward. It
missed Max by millimeters.

Max held on tightly to the bars. He looked
down. He was saw nothing but blackness. The

sound of the attacking spaceship faded into the distance. He waited a good five minutes before he threaded himself back out through the bars.

He saw with relief that the silver-and-purple craft was out of sight. He sprinted over to the door of the Zockran Command Center. Max pushed it open. He found himself in a long room. The room held chairs, desks, computer equipment, and digital screens.

Among this furniture were about fifty pale, silvery creatures scattered all over the floor. They were cylindrical in shape. There was no separation between their heads and their bodies. Each of them made small moaning sounds. Every time they moaned, their bodies rose a few inches off the ground. They fell to the floor again.

Max couldn't help staring.

These guys have nearly reached their sell-by date.

One of the creatures was larger than the others. He beckoned Max over to him with a long red finger.

"Max Flash," he wheezed. "I am Nineth—Ruler of Zockra. You have arrived just in time to save us. Please climb into one of the Pods. They're stationed in that room over there."

With great effort, Nineth lifted his finger. He pointed to a green door at the far side of the room.

"We will activate the Pod," said Nineth weakly. "The Aura Energy you transfer will give us the boost we need long before the machine reaches the Critical Point. You will re-energize us. You will suffer no harm yourself."

Max helped Nineth towards the door, and they passed through it. In front of them was a row of Re-Energizing Pods. They looked just like the one Zavonne had shown him. Each one was covered with dozens of tiny, flickering yellow lights.

"The DFEA has told me that it will not be safe for you to be in there any longer than two minutes," said Nineth.

"Do you think that will be long enough to re-energize you all?" Max asked.

Nineth nodded. "We cannot risk your safety, Max," he replied. "There is so much else for you to do."

Max opened the door of the first Pod. He

stepped inside. He watched as Nineth pressed a switch on the outside of the Pod.

Immediatelys a low humming sound started up. Max felt as if his whole body was being prodded by gentle fingers. It

wasn't an unpleasant experience. It certainly didn't hurt. As soon as two minutes were up, Nineth deactivated the Pod. The humming and the strange sensation stopped.

Max saw that the Pod could only be opened from the outside. He waited for Nineth to let him out.

Even with this short burst of Aura Energy, Nineth looked much better. Together, they returned to the main room of the Command Center. Everywhere, Zockrans were very slowly getting to their feet. Their features were far more clearly defined. The moaning had stopped, but they still looked very weak.

"Thank you," said Nineth. "We badly needed that Aura Energy."

"How long do you think it will last?" asked Max.

"It's hard to tell. We're used to ten people re-energizing us at one time. You must hurry and find the DFEA Unit."

"I know," Max said. "Have you got any idea who kidnapped them?"

Nineth was about to reply. Then he spotted something over Max's shoulder.

"I don't know exactly who they are. But that is definitely their spaceship!" he hissed.

Max spun around.

Out a large window he could see the silver-and-purple craft that had nearly mown him down. It was hovering in space about a hundred meters away.

"That's them!" said Nineth angrily. "They are our attackers. They have kidnapped the DFEA Unit!"

CHAPTER 9

Before Max could say anything, the silver-
and-purple craft suddenly boosted its rocket
cylinders. It started flying away from Zockra.

"Where are your spaceships?" asked Max.
"I have to go after them!"

"We haven't used spaceships for years,"
Nineth replied, shaking his head sadly. "Fuel
is in very short supply on Zockra. We use the
Hoppers or the Splook Tunnel to get around."

"The *what* tunnel?"

"The Splook Tunnel. It leads you onto the

Ballistic Highway. There's an Entry Port over there."

"Great," said Max, "How do you travel in this tunnel? Do you have some kind of special cars?"

"Some people do," said Nineth, "but we Zockrans prefer to walk."

"To WALK!" Max exclaimed.

"Yes. It may take you several thousand years to reach your destination. The Service Stations have excellent and quite reasonably priced menus."

Max groaned, but then he remembered the Board he had been given by Hunter.

Max yelled goodbye to Nineth. He sprinted to the Entry Port. He quickly pressed the button on the underside of the Zing-Board. It exploded into a full-sized board. The engine roared to life. Max dropped it onto the floor. Flames spat out of the exhaust.

Max took a deep breath. He jumped onto

the Board. It whirred ferociously. Its wheels buzzed. The whole Board went a deep, fizzing scarlet color. It then catapulted Max forward at the speed of sound. He went straight onto the madness that was the Ballistic Highway.

CHAPTER 10

The wind whipped past Max's face as the Zing-Board zipped forward. He whooped with exhilaration. Normal skateboarding was nothing compared to this! This wasn't just fast. This was supersonic! He wobbled dangerously. The Board took a sharp corner. He managed to keep his balance.

What a ride!

Max was traveling on one of several hundred lit tracks that twisted and curved in every direction.

Moving along these tracks were giant steel cubes with square wheels. They gave off millions of sparks. There were small, one-wheeled oval craft that looked like old-fashioned bathtubs on wheels. There was what looked like a yellow school bus. Except all of the aliens were traveling on the roof of the carriage. They were playing some sort of game using a crusty sluglike thing as a ball.

Max became used to the feeling of traveling at this ridiculously fast speed. He began to think about his destination, or in this case, his lack of destination. He realized he didn't have a clue where he was going. He didn't know if he was traveling in the same direction as the purple-and-silver spaceship.

I need to get a plan together. And quickly!

In the next instant, he was faced with a much bigger problem. A massive orange beast with a flat head and ten fiery red eyes came hurtling down the Splook Tunnel in the wrong direction. It was heading straight for Max. This promised to be the collision of the millennium.

Max tried to twist his Zing-Board onto the path to his right. It wouldn't budge. He looked up and saw that the orange alien was almost upon him. It would smash him off the track!

Sparks were flying off the orange creature's body. As the wind screamed past Max's ears, he closed his eyes and . . .

MISSION2

CHAPTER 11

. . . felt a light tap on his shoulder.

Very slowly he opened his eyes.

The orange alien had managed to veer off
Max's track. It was speeding off to the right.
Traveling right beside him now was a creature
with a large, fat, bright-green body. It had a
long, thin, pink nose and three black eyes. Its
circular feet were resting on what looked like a
grey surfboard.

"Can I see your license, please?" it asked.

"Er, what?"

"Your Splook Tunnel license," it replied wearily. "We've been catching a lot of unlicensed kids on the Ballistic Highway recently, so we're doing spot checks."

I haven't got time for this!

"My license?" said Max desperately. "I haven't got it on me."

The inspector shot Max three very suspicious looks with its eyes. "Not another one!" it exclaimed.

"After I've finished my business," said Max, "I'll zip back and get it."

The creature shook its head firmly. "I'm sorry, but I'm going to have to take you in."

"No!" pleaded Max. "I'm on an urgent mission to help the Zockrans."

The inspector's expression suddenly softened. "The Zockrans?"

Max nodded.

"Well, that's a different matter. What are you doing for them? I've heard that they're in

trouble. Are you here to help?"

Max heaved a sigh of relief. Maybe this alien could help him?

"I'm following a purple-and-silver ship that attacked planet Zockra," Max explained, "but I don't quite know where it's heading."

"Well, you're in luck. I know exactly where it's going. I pulled it over to check the paperwork earlier today. It's heading for Feronda."

"Feronda?" repeated Max.

The inspector nodded. "I stopped you just in time," it said, "we're very near the turnoff."

A minute later, the inspector pointed to a circular Entry Point that was looming up on them. It waited until they were almost parallel with it. Then it threw a small grey pellet down onto Max's Zing-Board. The pellet let off a shower of sparks before suddenly forcing the Board off the track. It shot it towards the Entry Point.

In a second, Max was through the Point. He flew straight down a ramp onto a paved walkway. He leaned back on the Board. It stopped abruptly with a ferocious squealing sound.

As he jumped off, the Board spluttered for a few seconds. Then it completely disintegrated.

Shame—everyone at school would have been impressed with that!

Max scanned his surroundings. The walkway was about one hundred and fifty feet wide. It stretched up a steep hill towards a huge ball of white light in the distance.

The light seemed to be coming out of a building up ahead.

Max was jostled by a group of rowdy green serpentlike creatures. After steadying himself he quickly checked the sky. There were lots of spacecraft up there, but absolutely no sign of the silver-and-purple one.

Where is it, who is on it, and what exactly

*am I going to do when I track them down?
Time's running out! I HAVE to recover that
DFEA Unit soon or the Zockrans won't survive!*

Max turned to the closest creature. It was a
female alien with an indigo body and a plump red
head.

"Good evening," he politely greeted her,
thankful again for the SPT device in his ear.
"Can you tell me where this walkway leads
to?"

She smiled warmly at Max. Then she slapped
him in the face.

CHAPTER 12

Max jolted backward.

"What was that for?" he shouted. He rubbed his sore cheek.

She grinned toothily. She whacked him again.

He hopped out of her way. Max held up his arms for protection.

"It's a traditional greeting when you meet an out-of-towner around here," she explained.

A second later, all sorts of aliens were streaming over to Max. They were slapping,

whacking, and flicking him.

"OK!" Max yelled. "You've all made this out-of-towner feel very welcome. Now will someone please tell me WHERE WE'RE ALL GOING?"

All of Max's slapping well-wishers suddenly stood back.

"To the Stadium of Power, of course!" replied the female alien. "It's the Feronda Festival!"

The alien looked surprised that Max hadn't heard of it.

"The Feronda Festival is the biggest event of its kind," she said. "People travel from all over the galaxy to watch it. There are hundreds of shows. There is magic, illusion, music, drama, and more. But most of us are going to see the Showcase Battles."

"Sounds like fun," replied Max. "But you haven't seen a silver-and-purple spaceship, have you? I know it's coming to Feronda. But I can't see it anywhere."

"Silver and purple?" she repeated.

Max nodded.

Her cheerful expression was replaced with a frown. "I have heard a strange rumor about a spaceship matching that description," she declared.

"What is it?" asked Max intently.

She leaned in toward him. She lowered her voice. "People are saying the craft belongs to an alien race. They have only just thawed out after being trapped in ice for many, many years."

"Why were they trapped? And who trapped them?" asked Max.

"That's all I know," she replied.

Did the Zockrans trap these creatures in ice? Is that what the kidnapping is all about— paying the Zockrans back by taking away their source of Aura Energy? And if it was the Zockrans, why didn't Nineth mention it? Surely he would know about such an incident?

Max was so busy puzzling over this new information that at first he didn't notice the crowd slowing down. Suddenly he realized he'd reached the stadium. He passed through a huge archway.

He looked up. He was standing at the bottom of a giant staircase that swooped upwards towards the sky. He turned around to thank the alien for her helpful information. But she'd been swept somewhere else by the crowd.

Max felt himself carried forward to the very top of the stairs. At the last step, he gasped. His eyes took in the most remarkable spectacle he'd ever seen.

CHAPTER 13

There was a huge sports stadium. It had
massive banks of spectators facing down
toward the oval field. Dazzling lights lit up
the stadium. In the crowd sat some of the
weirdest aliens Max had ever seen.

There were spindly blue creatures with
three bulging heads. There were square,
metallic beasts. These had tiny red heads
with twisting gold antennae. There were short
green monsters with no heads. These had five
eyes in the middle of their chests.

I need to track down the silver-and-purple ship. I need more info on the aliens flying it. Who are they? And why have they kidnapped the DFEA Unit?

A finger prodded his arm. "Do you want me to show you to your seat?" asked a yellow-spotted alien. The alien carried official programs. And it had a tray of disgusting-looking snacks.

"Er, no thanks," Max replied, "I'm not planning to hang around. But I am on the lookout for a silver-and-purple spaceship. I think its owners might have just recovered from being frozen in ice. Does that ring any bells?"

A scaly purple tongue hung from the alien's mouth. It stood thinking about the question for a few seconds.

"I haven't seen the ship," it eventually replied. "But I believe the species you talk of are called the Guzzlets. They have indeed woken up from a long ice sleep."

"Do you know who froze them?" asked Max.

"Of course," said the alien, "it was the Earthlings."

"Really?" gasped Max nervously. He felt his cheeks go a deep shade of red. "Earthlings, you say?"

"Yes," it answered. It suddenly arched its head forward. It was studying Max's face very closely. "Why are you so interested?"

"Er, it's a school project," Max replied weakly. "I'm late handing it in."

The creature moved even closer. Suddenly a spark of recognition came over its face.

"Surely not . . . " it muttered. Its eyes widened.

Max felt anxious. He was keen to get away from this alien. But it had grabbed him.

"YOU'RE an Earthling. Aren't you?" it asked. "I remember seeing a picture of your race hundreds of years ago when I was just a young alien."

"You're making a mistake!" said Max. "Just let me go!"

Max tried to free himself. The creature roared, "WE HAVE AN EARTHLING HERE!"

Chaos exploded. Aliens were on their feet. They were staring and pointing at Max. Their mouths gaped open (in some cases seven per creature). They were shouting "EARTHLING!" at the tops of their voices.

Before Max could react, hundreds of hands, claws, and feelers pushed and pulled him down. He struggled to break free. But it was no good. He was dragged down the seemingly endless row of steps. Dragged toward the field.

CHAPTER 14

"NO!" shouted Max desperately. He crashed downward. "Let me go! I'm on a special mission. I mean you no harm!"

His words were lost in the rising hysteria of the crowd. A minute later he was pushed over the side and onto the field. He stumbled a few paces backward. He looked wildly up at the towering stands above him. Thousands of alien eyes were gaping at him. Thousands of alien voices were shrieking "EARTHLING!" It was terrifying.

Suddenly, a giant shadow spread over the stadium. Max looked up. The silver-and-purple spaceship hovered right above the field.

"Your cries have alerted us to the fact that you have an Earthling down there," boomed a deep voice. "Can you confirm?"

"Confirmed," answered a machine somewhere in the stadium.

Max was rooted to the spot. He stared up at the giant craft.

"Permission to land?" said the deep voice.

"Permission granted."

So this is when I finally get to meet these Guzzlets. I can start trying to get the DFEA Unit released. I can't believe Zavonne didn't warn me about them!

The ship began its descent. It stopped about a hundred meters above the field.

"WELCOME TO THE TWO HUNDRED AND TWENTY-SIX THOUSANDTH FERONDA

FESTIVAL!" screeched a tinny voice. "AND WHAT AN UNEXPECTED, LAST-MINUTE TREAT WE HAVE IN STORE FOR YOU. FOR THIS YEAR'S FIRST SHOWCASE BATTLE I GIVE YOU TWO OF HISTORY'S MOST BITTER RIVALS. IN THE LEFT CORNER, WE HAVE A REAL HUMAN EARTHLING. IN THE RIGHT CORNER ARE TWO VICIOUS ICE MEN—THE GUZZLETS. LET'S GET READY TO RUUUUUUUUUUUUUMBLE!"

The crowd erupted with excitement.

Max swallowed anxiously. He made a scary calculation.

Spaceship filled with human-hating Guzzlets + crowd roaring in excitement = extremely serious trouble.

Two holes appeared on the underside of the spaceship. Two steel ladders shot out. A second later, two huge creatures emerged. The creatures climbed down onto the field. They had silver-and-purple-striped

bodies and powerful arms. Their heads were triangular. Each had three glaring eyes. Their mouths were full of metal teeth that snapped like shredders. They each had two thin, flamingolike legs. Max noticed that their bodies were covered in a thick layer of ice. Sub-zero wind stream surrounded them. Max caught the chilly air on his face. He shivered.

"FIGHT! FIGHT! FIGHT!" chanted the crowd.

The massive Guzzlets took a few steps foward.

"Your people trapped us in ice for hundreds of years," one boomed. "Now it's time for our revenge!"

"Can't we just talk this over?" Max suggested. He slowly backed away from the menacing aliens.

But a chat was the last thing on the Guzzlets' minds. Without any warning, a purple tentacle shot out from the first one's stomach. It flung Max backward. He crashed

against one of the billboards. Another tentacle lashed out from the second Guzzlet. It curled around Max's head. He suddenly felt the blood draining out of him. He used all of his strength to wrench the tentacle off him. He thwacked the tentacle to the ground. The Guzzlet snorted furiously. The crowd booed.

If I don't get out of here soon, I'll be smashed.

A third tentacle whipped out from the first alien. It was followed by a fourth tentacle from the second alien. They lifted Max thirty feet in the air. Then they hurled him backward again. He thudded onto the field. He struggled to his feet. The Guzzlets roared victoriously. They came stamping toward Max.

He gulped. He desperately wished he still had the Zing-Board.

Wait! The Net Can!

Max pulled the gadget out of his pocket. To his horror, the ice coming off the Guzzlets had made his fingers cold. He couldn't activate the ring pull.

"NOOOOOOOOOOOOOOOOOOOOOOOO!" yelled Max.

CHAPTER 15

One of the Guzzlets reached out. It snatched
the can. It turned it toward Max and pulled
the ring.

Immediately, a huge net shot out. It circled
Max's body and tied itself very tightly around
him. The crowd roared. The Guzzlets looked at
each other with mouths wide open. They both
roared with laughter.

Max stood there, feeling ridiculous. He'd
been captured with one of his own gadgets.
That wasn't supposed to happen!

A few feet away, the Guzzlets were loving every moment. They waved at the crowd. They bowed. The roars got louder, and they puffed up their chests. They threw their arms in the air and set off on a lap of honor.

Max got to work. He knew this was his one chance. He only had a few seconds to get it right.

When the rope had shot over him, he had squeezed both of his hands into the space where the knot tied itself. This gave him a small circle of space to work in. He lost no time. He twisted and pushed out his wrists. His hands worked the gap. Slowly, the rope started to give. He took a quick glance at the Guzzlets. They were still bowing and waving.

The opening in the net was nearly big enough. He gave it one more twist. He compressed his body. He started to push out through the hole.

In ten seconds, he was out.

The crowd screamed in alarm. The two
Guzzlets spun round.

"Sorry, boys. I can't hang around!" shouted

Max. He ran off at full speed toward the other side of the field.

The Guzzlets chased after him. As Max ran, he felt tentacles shooting out at his back. He sidestepped some. He whacked the others aside. But they were gaining on him. He fought out in every direction. He was desperate to stop them wrapping around his body and squeezing him to death.

And then something terrible happened.

The Guzzlets sprang forward. They flew over the top of Max. They came crashing down about sixty feet in front of him. They turned to face him. Their faces were filled with hate.

Max made a snap decision.

There's only one way I'm going to get out of here alive.

Instead of running away from the Guzzlets, he raced straight toward them. He picked up speed. And he suddenly dove to the ground.

He crashed forward on his knees. The Guzzlets leaned down to try and grab him. Their bodies were too big to react quickly. Max skidded over the turf. He careened right between one of the Guzzlets' legs and out a door in the stadium wall.

Three tiny yellow aliens with star-shaped heads jumped in fright. Beyond them was some sort of space park. It had a single red ship parked against a large white wall.

Max blocked out the howls of rage from the stadium. He sped toward the red ship. Its walkway was open. A pink-colored alien with a long pointy head and six chunky arms stood outside. It paged through a newspaper.

Max ran straight up the walkway.

"Hey!" shouted the alien. But Max barged past it. He sped through a metal door at the far end of the walkway. He slammed the door shut. Max heard the pink creature pounding on the door.

Max bolted the door and turned around. He found himself on the ship's flight deck. It was empty. He sprinted over to the huge control desk. He checked out the hundreds of buttons and switches.

I have to free that DFEA team before the Guzzlets get to me. They must be planning a revenge attack on Earth. We need the protection of the Zockrans!

A large black button on the desk declared ENGINE IGNITE.

Sounds good.

Max was about to press it when he felt something cold and steely against his cheek. He turned around. He found himself staring straight into the barrel of a giant silver gun.

CHAPTER 16

A very tall, thin alien held the gun. Its dark green skin was stretched tight on its body. It had two heads, each with one massive eye.

"Who are you that dares break into a Thargon Commander's ship?" demanded the angry creature.

"I'm SO sorry," smiled Max weakly. He was not sure which head he should be speaking to. "I didn't realize you were a Commander. I just thought you were an average Thargon."

Max heard shouts and stampeding feet outside the ship.

It's the Guzzlets, plus whoever else wants to see me pummeled!

Max felt sweat running down his forehead. Before the Thargon Commander could do anything, Max reached across and pressed the ENGINE IGNITE button. The roaring sound of engines exploded. The ship leaped upward.

The Commander clicked off the safety on the gun.

"What's going on, sir?" shouted a voice at the back of the flight deck.

Two more Thargons stood in the doorway. Their weapons were aimed at Max.

One gun facing me isn't ideal, but three?

Then Max saw a circular yellow panel on the floor. He realized what he had to do. As the three Thargons closed in on him, Max retreated. He stepped back until he reached the circular panel on the deck. The Thargons didn't take their eyes off him. A second later, they too had unknowingly stepped into the circle.

Max hurled himself into the air. He somersaulted over the aliens' heads, kicking

out and activating a wall button labeled EJECT.

A roof panel flipped open. The Thargons were shot straight out. A fierce blast of air tried to steer Max out too. But he clung tightly to a steel bar. A couple of seconds later, the roof panel closed.

Max let go of the bar. He dropped back down onto the deck.

On the viewing screen he watched as the shocked and furious Thargons fell back down to Feronda.

Max jumped down onto a high-backed chair. He took a closer look at the control desk. There were hundreds of buttons and levers on the desk. Only a few were marked with signs.

Luckily, Max recognized the symbol for throttle. He hit it. The Thargon spaceship started increasing its speed.

I need to get to the Guzzlets' home planet. But how am I going to find it?

He pulled out the interstellar map. He

studied the Hedra galaxy. He scanned the stars and moons. He spotted a tiny planet faintly marked with the word *Guzzle*.

Yes!

Max couldn't help smiling to himself.

I know where I'm heading now. Full speed ahead!

But a second later, the smile was erased from his face. The Thargon spaceship took a direct hit from a thunderous missile.

Max shielded his face with his arms. His body thudded against a rack of equipment. He was thrown to the deck.

He staggered to his feet. Max ran to the control desk.

In the viewing screen he saw the silver-and-purple Guzzlet ship. An orange flame exploded from its underside. Another missile powered its way towards the Thargon craft. The Guzzlets were hoping to destroy him.

Max lunged for the controls. But he was too

late. The missile smashed into the front of the Thargon ship. Max was knocked off his feet again.

I need to hit back!

Max stumbled back to the desk. He searched frantically for a MISSILE LAUNCH sign. He couldn't find one. Another flame burst from the Guzzlet ship. Another missile was on its way.

He looked around desperately. He noticed a red lever on the far right-hand side of the control desk.

Give it a go! I've got nothing to lose!

The Guzzlet missile screeched closer. Max yanked the lever down to the left. Miraculously, the Thargon ship crashed to the left. The Guzzlet missile whistled past. It exploded in a fireball somewhere behind the Thargon ship.

You missed that time, suckers!

But two more Guzzlet missiles had already launched. Max grabbed the lever. He steered

the Thargon ship between the incoming
rockets. His directional skill was perfect. He
just managed to miss both missiles.

*I'm getting the hang of this! It's like playing
a computer game.*

Another Guzzlet rocket launched. Max tilted
his ship to the right, narrowly avoiding a hit.
But Max noticed a turquoise light flashing
on the control desk. It signaled that fuel was
running low.

Now is NOT a good time to run out of fuel!

Max stared at the viewing screen. He could
see a row of bombs at the rear of the Guzzlet
ship.

I'll be a sitting target!

He scanned the space outside his viewing
screen. He noticed a series of dense dust
clouds. There were at least twenty of them.

Max pulled the lever to the right. The
Thargon ship lurched towards the dust clouds.
A few more seconds and it had dipped behind

the first one. He moved swiftly behind the second and third clouds. He came to rest behind the fourth. It was a risky strategy. But he didn't have another one.

He studied the viewing screen. The Guzzlet ship was out of sight.

But it won't be long before they come hunting for me.

He nudged the lever. He took the Thargon ship behind the fifth, sixth, seventh, then eighth cloud. He waited for a minute. Nothing happened.

He nosed the front of the Thargon ship a tiny bit forward. He quickly pulled back as he saw the Guzzlet craft loom into view.

Another minute went by. He snatched another look out of the viewing screen. The Guzzlets were starting to move off. They were going pretty slowly and cautiously. But it was definitely in the opposite direction.

Max breathed a deep sigh of relief.

Safe . . . at least for the moment.

He cruised out from behind the eighth dust cloud. He looked out at the orange taillights of the Guzzlet spaceship. He flicked the CABIN LIGHTS OFF button. Immediately the Thargon ship descended into darkness. The flight deck was illuminated only by the thousands of tiny lights on the control desk. Max touched the lever. The ship floated forward. He needed to keep the Guzzlets in his sights while making sure that they didn't see him.

He knew what he had to do. He had to follow the Guzzlets until they led him to planet Guzzle. Then he needed to find the DFEA Unit. But time was rapidly slipping away. He was more aware than ever that the Zockrans' survival completely depended on him.

He was absolutely certain that "failure" was not a word in Zavonne's vocabulary. He couldn't return to Earth until the DFEA

Unit had been found, the Zockrans properly
re-energized, and his planet protected from
possible attacks once more.

CHAPTER 18

Max trailed the Guzzlet ship. He noticed
a sudden drop in the air temperature. He
shivered and checked the ship's temperature
gauge. The needle was quickly moving into
negative territory. Up ahead, he watched as
the Guzzlet ship began to descend. It was
dipping towards a planet completely covered
in ice.

This must be planet Guzzle—at last!

The cold was sweeping through the flight
deck. It was biting at Max's face and hands

just as it had when he'd faced the Guzzlet
warriors in the stadium.

Max followed the Guzzlet ship from a safe
distance. He watched it land. He waited until
all of those onboard had exited. They headed
into a tall building near the landing pad.

*What will it be like outside? Will my
spacesuit give me enough protection to
survive even a very short period out in that
hostile climate?*

Max began a slow, smooth descent. With
every meter, the temperature dropped. He felt
his spaceship crunch onto the ice below. He
turned off the engine.

He flicked the switch to unlock the door. He
heard a loud click. A hatch on the left-hand
side of the flight deck opened. Max flipped on
his space helmet. He walked outside, not sure
what to expect.

The chill hit him like a powerful punch.

It was freezing multiplied by a million.

The cold felt like a thousand knife points on Max's body. His teeth were chattering violently.

Wherever he looked, there was ice. No wonder the Guzzlets wanted revenge against Earth for forcing them to live in these conditions for so long. Max spotted a large building through the swirling mist. He struggled towards it. He made a mental note. Never, ever complain again when it was a bit cold on a school morning. Compared to this, that would be a beach vacation in the Bahamas.

Even though he was wearing his helmet, his eyes were crusted with ice. His ears felt like they were about to snap off his head. Finally, he reached the building's white front door. He reached out a hand. He just about managed to grab the handle.

No sooner had he done that than a robotic voice called out, "Enter your password."

In shock Max spotted the small entry panel beside the door.

"Enter your password," repeated the voice. "If no password is entered after this third prompt, security will be called immediately."

Max began to panic. Summoning security was not very high on his wish list.

He needed inspiration.

But none came.

"Calling security in five seconds," announced the voice. "Five, four, three . . . "

CHAPTER 19

"Hang . . . hang on a sec," spluttered Max, his teeth chattering violently.

"Two," said the voice.

"STOP!" shouted Max.

The voice went silent.

"Thanks," said Max.

"No one's ever interrupted my countdown before," huffed the voice.

"Sorry about that," answered Max. "But I don't have the password. I really need to get inside."

"No password, no entry," retorted the voice sharply.

Come on Max, think, think! Maybe flattery will work . . . ?

"I really admire you," said Max. He tried to stop his body from shivering.

A pause. "Why is that?" asked the voice.

"Well, it must take a supremely intelligent lifeform to operate an entry system."

"You can tell I'm supremely intelligent?" inquired the voice hopefully.

"It's obvious!" cried Max. "Your voice has intelligence all over its electronic vocal cords."

The voice let out a giggle. "No one has ever praised me before," it gushed. "It's wonderful to finally be appreciated."

"But I suppose," continued Max, "your powers don't stretch to knowing anything about what goes on inside this building?"

"Yes, they do!" protested the voice. "I know *everything*!"

"I bet you don't know the location of the DFEA Unit."

"Of course I do!" replied the voice. "They're being kept in the strong room on the outer southern wall of this complex."

"Wow," said Max. He was desperate to get out of the cold. "That is very impressive. But I need to get in now."

"Are you sure you don't want to know anything else?" The voice sounded a bit disappointed.

"Not for the moment, thanks," smiled Max. "But I'll spread the word about your amazing abilities."

"Would you?" said the voice, perking up. "That would be great."

And with that, the door clicked open. A very cold but very relieved Max Flash entered the building.

The warmth hit him immediately. He stood there for several minutes. He thawed out his

hands and feet.

He was in a long, narrow corridor. He began
to run down it, wincing. His feet felt like
oversized blocks of ice. Each step he took,
although painful, restored some feeling to
them. Max spotted a sliding door. He peered
around it. He saw a large square room bathed
in silver-and-purple light.

Max grinned. Standing against the wall were
ten humans wearing shiny orange suits. The
suits had DFEA across the front in silver letters.

I've made it!

The Unit had five men and five women. Each of them was smiling and waving at Max. He waved back and started striding across the room towards them.

"Hey guys!" He beamed.

But in that instant, the ten members of the DFEA Unit completely vanished.

CHAPTER 20

What's going on?

Max looked at the empty space where the Unit had been. He shook his head. They'd been there. He'd seen them with his own eyes. They hadn't been cardboard cutouts. They'd been real living, breathing humans. So where were they?

He grappled with this mysterious twist. Then suddenly, twenty panels on the walls of the room slid open. A Guzzlet marched through each one.

"Welcome to planet Guzzle!" said the largest and ugliest alien. "A freezing, perilous dungeon!"

It's always great to hear someone talking up their home planet!

"I don't plan on taking a vacation here," replied Max. "Shall we cut to the chase? I've come to release the DFEA Unit."

"I'm surprised one so clever as you fell for our fake projections of your cronies," hissed the Guzzlet Chief. "You can work wonders with a Multi-Cryptonic Slide Projector."

"How very clever of you. Now if you don't mind, I'll just get the Unit. We'll leave you and your Slide Projector alone."

"Oh dear!" the Chief sighed dramatically. "You are so out of your depth here, it's frightening. I almost feel sorry for you."

"The only thing that's frightening is your breath!" exclaimed Max. "I can smell it from here. Have you been drinking from a sewage pipe?"

The Guzzlet Chief spat out a huge blob of liquid that hissed. It sizzled on the floor before burning itself out.

"You can mock all you like," sneered the Chief. "But nothing will stop us from getting revenge on your people. You stopped our plans for total intergalactic domination by freezing us. Our time has now come. With the Zockrans out of action, we can attack your pathetic little planet. We can make you all Guzzlet slaves. It's about time us Guzzlets took a nice, long holiday. Your planet has all those beaches, cities, and mountains. It looks PERFECT!" He laughed at the look of horror on Max's face. He snapped his fingers.

Max looked up. He saw some sort of contraption being lowered toward him on a thin metal pulley. As it got nearer, he recognized it.

It was a Re-Energizing Pod.

The Guzzlet Chief shot Max a gruesome

smile. "In just over two minutes, you won't have the energy to save the day! Your rescue mission will be over!"

Max's brain whirred. The Guzzlets must have stolen one of the pods along with the DFEA crew. Now he was about to have all his Aura Energy drained out of him. He had to do something fast!

MAX FLASH MISSION 2

CHAPTER 21

Max did not try to run. He walked calmly up to the door. He let himself in.

"A willing victim?" noted the Chief, puzzled.

But Max had just hatched a plan.

It would require several elements to work at the same time. But it was possible.

"Strange. But no matter!" cried the Guzzlet Chief. He threw his hands in the air. "IT'S SHOWTIME!"

The Chief walked over and hit the Activate switch on the outside of the Pod. Max immediately felt the sensations he'd experienced when he'd re-energized the Zockrans back on Zockra. The Guzzlets clapped their hands and roared approval. Max reached inside one of the pockets of his spacesuit.

Max knew he had a short space of time to make this plan work. He knew he had to leave the Pod immediately after two minutes were up. Max didn't want to be inside this thing when the Critical Point was reached.

He brought out the Direct Passage Pulverizer. He pulled out a short length of tape.

Holding the roll in one hand, he reached out and stuck the tape to the front of the Pod. There was a huge spark of electricity. The Pod crashed forward at blistering speed. It smashed through the wall in front of it.

"STOP HIM!" shrieked the Chief as great chunks of rubble flew through the air. The noise was deafening. But the Pod had only just

started its journey. It sped through another room. It clattered through the wall at its far side. Max pushed his arms against the wall of the Pod to steady himself.

But his relief at this blistering escape was suddenly overtaken by a weird sensation that was suddenly spreading through his body. It was as if hundreds of little sharp forks were pricking him.

I must be nearing the Critical Point!

Still, the Pod continued on its frenzied path. It bashed through a third, a fourth, and a fifth room. It left a devastating trail of bricks, stone, and dust in its wake. Max stole a backward glance. Through the great haze, Max could see the Guzzlet Chief and his orderlies running behind him.

The stabbing was getting sharper now. Max's brain was beginning to feel pinched and tight.

I have to get out of here soon!

The Pod sped on, leaving a vast hole in every wall it ripped through.

Max felt his brain going all fuzzy. It was as if concrete was being tipped inside his head. His eyelids became incredibly heavy. He sensed he was losing consciousness.

Must stay awake. Must. Get. Out . . .

The Pod flew through the seventh room. Through his heavy eyes, Max spied a group of people huddled together in a corner. The Pod smashed through the far wall of the seventh room. This led to the outside and into the frozen wasteland. The Pod thudded over the ice and snow. It abruptly stopped.

The ten figures leaped to their feet. They ran toward him. The first of the figures to jump through the smashed wall was a woman with short brown hair. She hit the Deactivate switch on the outside of the Pod. Then she yanked open the door.

Max staggered a couple of steps forward. He

fell out of the Pod.

The woman caught him. "Operative Sandy Larsson," she said. "I head up this DFEA Unit."

Max felt as if a heavy blanket was being
pulled from his body and brain. The prodding
fork points seemed to vanish in the air. He
was delighted to see Larsson and the others.
He hardly noticed the freezing conditions this
time.

"Great to meet you," replied Max. He
stretched his arms out in front of him. He
shook his head to remove the last of the
strange sensations. "There's a Thargon
spaceship at the launch pad. You must fly
back to Zockra. The Zockrans desperately need
your Aura Energy. The ship is low on fuel.
Take some from the Guzzlets' craft before you
go."

"You're coming with us," Operative Larsson
said.

"I have some unfinished business here," he
replied. He jerked his thumb in the direction
of the Guzzlets, who were streaming through
the fifth room. They were nearly upon them.

"We can't leave you," said Larsson.

"YOU HAVE TO!" shouted Max. "I KNOW WHAT I'M DOING!"

Larsson and the other DFEA members exchanged uncertain looks.

"You're sure?" asked Larsson.

"Completely sure," replied Max. "PLEASE, GO NOW!"

Larsson nodded. She started running around the side of the building with her team right behind her. They were braving the swirling, icy mists and freezing temperature.

Max looked back at the fast approaching Guzzlets. He reached into his pocket and hauled out the Hopper Hurry Card. Time to take a little trip . . .

MISSION 2

CHAPTER 22

"You called, amigo?"

Max turned around. He saw the very welcome sight of Arcan in his Planet Hopper. Max grinned and yelled, "Hey, Arcan! That was quick. Can you open the carriage doors?"

Arcan pressed a button. The two doors slid open.

The Guzzlets were almost on top of Max now.

"In here, guys!" shouted Max. He ran through the first door into the carriage. The

Guzzlet Chief and his followers roared in anger. They piled straight into the carriage. Max sped down past the seats towards the carriage's other door. He looked back to make sure every Guzzlet was onboard. When he was satisfied they were all in, he shouted to Arcan.

"CLOSE THE DOORS!"

Max knew his timing had to be perfect.

The second door started to close. Max made his move. He threw himself forward. He just managed to slide through the gap before the door crashed shut.

Max had made it into Arcan's front carriage. He turned around. He stared into the carriage behind.

The Guzzlets were completely freaking out. They were dribbling and shrieking and banging on the carriage doors.

Max pulled out his interstellar map, studied it for a couple of seconds, and then told Arcan where to go.

"No problemo!" laughed the alien, slamming his foot down. The Planet Hopper soared away from the freezing planet Guzzle. It arced upwards towards a bank of glittering stars.

"What have you been up to?" asked Arcan. "It looks like things have been getting seriously heavy."

"They have," said Max, "but it's nothing I can't handle."

They sped through the sky. The sound of the Hopper's engine competed with the screams of the Guzzlets in the carriage behind them.

"May I?" asked Max after a few minutes, indicating the driver's microphone.

"Go for it," beamed Arcan.

Max turned the microphone on. He cleared his throat.

"Lovely to have you Guzzlets onboard," Max said into the microphone. "We'll be traveling at six billion light-years per second. We will be arriving at our destination shortly. Look out for the yellow-tinged nebula to your left. You won't be seeing it again for quite some time."

Max could hear the moans and screeches of the locked-in Guzzlets.

"And don't forget to put any litter in the bins provided," added Max. "We don't want anyone messing up this marvelous transport system."

"You're a natural," laughed Arcan. "There are some Hopper driver's jobs open at the minute. Why not apply?"

Max grinned. "Maybe one day," he replied.

Arcan braked suddenly.

"I believe this is your selected destination," he announced to Max.

MISSION 2

CHAPTER 23

The Hopper screeched to a halt.

Max looked at the station sign just outside the driver's carriage.

DELTA BLACK HOLE 1713.

Arcan shrugged his shoulders. "What do you want to do with that lot back there?" he enquired.

Max spied a button labeled TILT in front of him.

He pressed DOORS OPEN and followed this with TILT.

The Hopper's two passenger doors slid open.
The train leaned steeply to the right.

The Guzzlets tumbled out of the carriage,
straight into the mouth of the black hole.

"NOOOOOOOOOOOOOOOOOOO!" shrieked
the Guzzlets. It was too late. They were already
being sucked down into the depths of the
swirling mass.

Max and Arcan did a high five. They both burst out laughing.

"You really showed those dudes," chuckled Arcan.

"I couldn't have done it without you," Max grinned.

"Where to next?" enquired Arcan.

"Back to planet Zockra!" shouted Max with relief.

Arcan flipped the Planet Hopper around. Within minutes they were back on Zockra. Max clambered out of the Hopper. He turned to say goodbye to Arcan. "Thanks for everything," he said.

"It's my pleasure," the friendly alien replied.

"If you're ever on Earth, I'll take you on a bus. It'll be a lot less cool than traveling in your Hopper, though!" said Max.

And with that, Arcan waved and zoomed off. Max waited until the silver taillights of the Hopper had disappeared over one of the six horizons in view. Then he started walking over to the Community Center.

On entering, he stopped in his tracks. He was amazed at the transformation of the room. The Zockrans were buzzing around the place. They were no longer pale, frail, and desperately ill.

I did it! thought Max. *I saved them!*

Nineth picked his way through the crowds and reached Max's side.

"Welcome back," he smiled, his face looking far more alive than before. "Your colleagues from the DFEA are currently sleeping after their experiences. They were hoping to be up to bid you farewell. Zavonne is keen for you to return immediately. I've arranged for your spaceship to be brought here from the Hedra Docking Station." Nineth placed his hands on Max's shoulders. "Your bravery will never be forgotten on Zockra," he declared.

"Glad to be of service," Max said proudly.

CHAPTER 24

Max was back in the spaceship. He was heading home. He went over everything that had happened on his mission to the Hedra galaxy.

No one at school would believe even the tiniest fraction of it!

It had been a crazy trip. Max suddenly felt very sleepy. His eyes began to close. He would have slept the whole journey back if it hadn't been for the loud voice booming out from the flight panel.

"THROTTLE OVERRIDE! SHUTTLE TRAVELING AT UNACCEPTABLE SPEED! ACTIVATE BRAKES."

Max opened his eyes. He scanned the flight panel for a BRAKES control. It was nowhere to be seen.

"ACTIVATE BRAKES!" the voice repeated.

Max looked to his right at the ship's navigation screen. It showed their exact position. They were nearly upon Earth.

Max looked at the flight panel again.

Where are the brakes?

He gulped in horror.

If I don't stop this thing soon, I'll be dust.

Frantically, Max thought back to his session in the flight simulator with Hunter. He was sure Hunter had talked about the brakes. He couldn't recall where they were.

He checked the navigation screen again. The shuttle was rapidly going down. Earth was getting bigger and bigger.

"IMPACT IMMINENT!" announced the panel. "APPLY BRAKES IMMEDIATELY!"

Max threw himself against the flight panel. He pressed every single switch. He was desperate to stop the craft.

The brakes must be somewhere!

And then he saw it. A small foot pedal wedged quite a way in beneath the bottom of the panel. It had a narrow sign reading BRAKES.

What a ridiculous place to put it!

Max kicked his leg forward. He couldn't reach the pedal. He kicked out again, but still without luck.

"DANGER OF DEATH! DANGER OF DEATH!" boomed the panel voice.

Max looked at the navigation screen. He could see the DFEA Space Base rapidly approaching.

In a last, desperate attempt to avoid death, Max pulled his leg back and threw himself onto

his front. He squashed his body down against the floor. He wriggled forward under the flight panel. He managed to get further than his leg had stretched, but even this wasn't far enough.

"CRASH SITUATION! CRASH SITUATION!" bellowed the panel.

Straining every muscle, Max made one last attempt to activate the brakes. He just managed to catch the edge of the panel with his hand.

The spaceship came to a violent halt. It caused Max to bang his head on the underside of the panel. He winced in pain. He slowly pulled himself out. He stared in horror at the navigation screen. The craft was hanging no more than one hundred and fifty feet above the opening hatch on top of the Space Base.

If he'd been a fraction of a second later, he wouldn't have made it.

MAX FLASH MISSION2

Max guided the spacecraft into the docking station. He breathed a huge sigh of relief.

Hunter was waiting at the bottom of the stairs. He had a very concerned expression on his face.

"I can't believe there was a throttle override," said Hunter when Max reached the bottom of the steps.

"I can't believe the brakes were so hard to get to!" replied Max.

Hunter frowned. "That must have been Operative Dawson. He's got very long legs.

He must have moved the pedal to suit his frame."

"Er, why didn't you check that out before you sent me up there?"

Hunter scratched his ear and looked embarrassed. "Time was tight. I couldn't cover every base. Looks like you did OK up there, though! Change out of the spacesuit. I'll take you to where your father is waiting. We contacted him when news of your return came through on the monitor. He's anxious to see you."

Max pulled off the spacesuit with some regret. It was much cooler than his school uniform, that was for sure!

Hunter led Max back to the shrubs. The shrubs parted to reveal Max's dad's car parked by the side of the road.

"Well done, Max," said Hunter. He shook Max's hand.

Max's dad jumped out of the driver's seat. He

gave him a hug. "I want to know everything. First of all, are you OK?"

"I'm fine, Dad. It's great to be back in one piece!"

His dad steered the car back down the road. Max began a blow-by-blow account of his second DFEA operation. By the end of the hour-long journey, Max had told his dad pretty much everything.

His mom was waiting for them by the front door. They pulled up to the house. "Well done!" she beamed. "Zavonne wants to see you straight away."

She doesn't waste a second!

Max nodded. He headed down to the cellar. Back in the communications center, Zavonne's face was already on the plasma screen.

"You certainly cut it a bit close to save the Zockrans," she said coldly.

"I did it as fast as I could," Max replied.

Zavonne pursed her lips. "Operative

Larsson has filled me in on your escapade on Guzzle. So those Guzzlets were planning on invading Earth and enslaving us all?" she asked.

Max nodded. "You might have warned me about them! Anyway, I think I've put the Guzzlets out of action for a while," he smiled.

Zavonne's expression remained frosty. "Let's hope so. I trust you only used your gadgets in extremely dangerous situations?"

"Of course," Max replied.

"Then this debrief signals the successful end of your mission," noted Zavonne.

"Will there be another mission for me?"

Zavonne fixed him with her icy stare. "That remains to be seen."

Before Max could say anything else, the image of Zavonne fizzled out. The plasma screen turned blank.

Typical, thought Max. *Zavonne the ice queen would be right at home on planet Guzzle . . .*

EPILOGUE

In Black Hole 1713, as the Guzzlets were turning and spinning in the infinite blackness, one of them hesitantly made his way over to the Guzzlet Chief.

"I suppose we should look on the bright side," suggested the junior Guzzlet. "I mean, we were encased in ice for hundreds of years. We're used to being stuck in places with a terrible view."

The howls of the other Guzzlets could be heard in every galaxy within a one-hundred-million-mile radius.

IT'S TIME FOR MAX'S
THIRD TOP SECRET
MISSION . . .

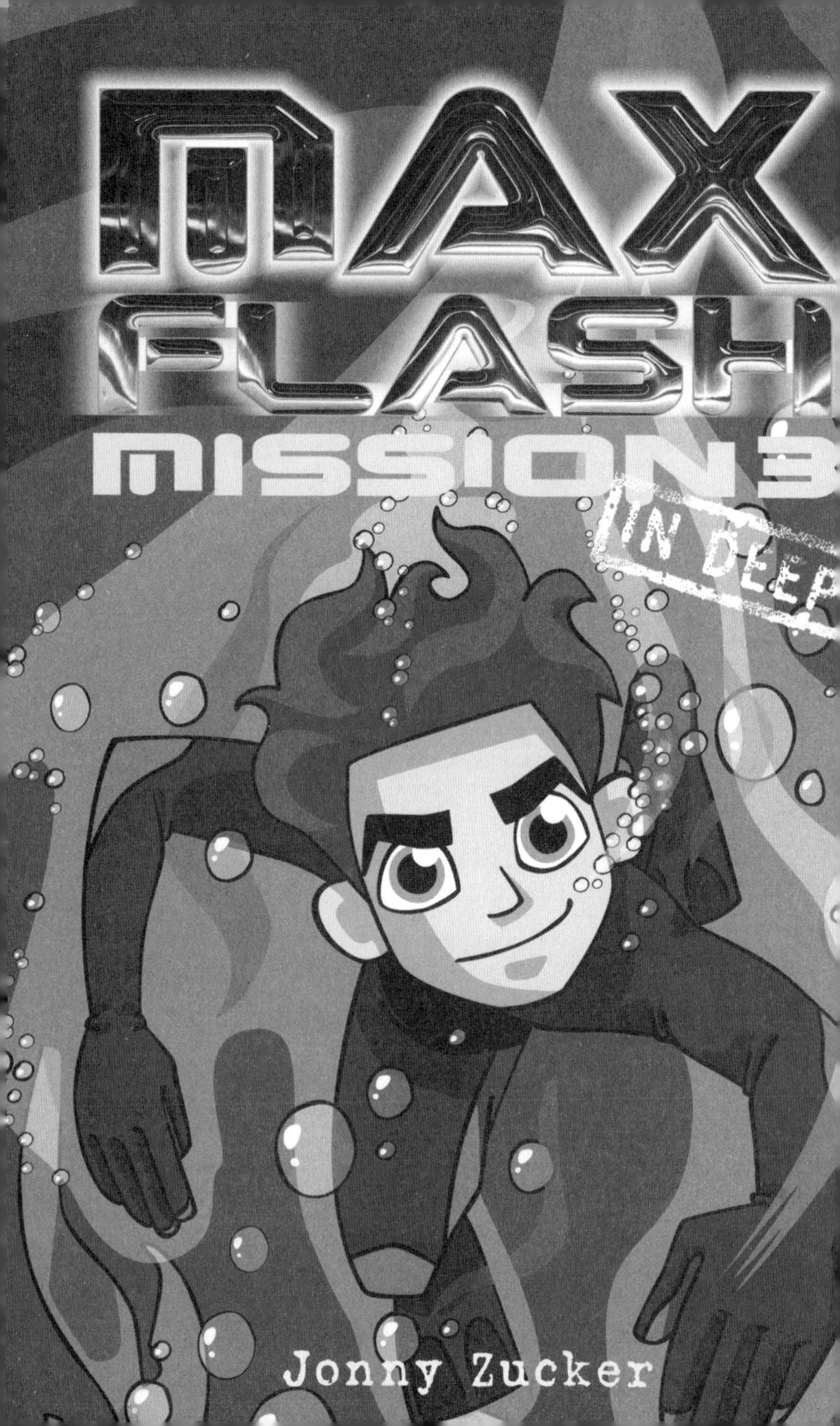
MAX FLASH
MISSION 3
IN DEEP
Jonny Zucker